Moral Tales No.3

The Painter

By

Sean De Siun

Published January2021
by Fileata Fiction.

This is the second in a series of short stories, Moral Tales.

A CIP record for this book is available
from National LIbrary of Australia

ISBN 978-0-6451139-0-7

COPY SALES
The Curator is available on **www.amazon.com**

Purchase direct and
Distribution enquiries:
Fileata Fiction
www.fileata.co
sales@fileata.co

1

The painter had been living in De Pijp district of Amsterdam for many years. For the last few years, he slept and cooked his meals in his studio. It was a large open space with a kitchen in one corner and a bed closet for him to sleep in. His wife lived a few streets away on Kuipersstraat in their family home, but he mostly only saw her on the weekends. His two children had grown up and left the city to work in London and Berlin.

He loved his wife, but it was his work, painting, that he felt an urgent need to concentrate on. He hated wasting a minute not thinking about, or working on a painting. With a growing sense of urgency, the painter wanted to complete his life's work while he was still able to.

As usual he awoke at 7 am, made breakfast and brewed his coffee. He wandered down the street to the local Albert Heijn store for food supplies. Then he sat down in front of his canvas and painted.

During the day he often had a break and strolled down Govert Flinckstraat the short distance to the Amstel and sat by the riverbank to watch the canal boats chug past and the cyclists pedal along the river bank.

Most afternoons he took a walk through the old city. Today as he set off there was a warm September breeze rustling through the full grown leaves of the plain trees on Stadhouderskade. The luscious aroma of late summer mixed with sea air and fragrant flowers tinged with the musty, sweet scent of hashish as he passed by the local coffee shop.

He loved the sounds of Amsterdam. The church and clock tower bells chiming throughout the day in singsong slightly off key melodies. The squeal of the trams as they scooted along their rails. The constant tinkle tinkle of bicycle bells as they gracefully glided along the streets in an almost constant stream.

He wandered into the Gracths crossing Singlegracht and continued into Centrum. He zigzagged along the canals crossing one bridge then walked left until he came to the next bridge, crossed that bridge and turned left again. After Single he crossed Lijnbaangracht, then Prinsen, Keizers and Herengrachts.

Now tired, he rested on a bench on Brouwersgracht and watched the world go by. The world really did go by. People from everywhere walked, cycled or floated by in canal cruisers with the tour guide describing the scene in Korean, Chinese or Italian.

Watching cyclists was his favourite pastime. People of all ages and dress cycled to and from work, the shops, bars and everywhere. Men in suits with their phones pressed to their ears. Mothers with babies in the cargo holds of their 'Bakfiets'. Women of all ages some dressed for the office or an evening out in high heels and revealing skirts. Casual young women, their hair flowing and bare legs in mini skirts or shorts pumped their pedals with such confidence and strength. The dynamism of the girls riding past him, rosy cheeks and serene expressions, the combination of movement and feminine beauty stirred him. To the painter these were the most beautiful sights in elegant, old, picturesque and lovely Amsterdam.

When he attended art school and for many years after, he went to figure drawing and painting sittings. But now he didn't need them, he just watched the cyclists and people going about their daily lives and that gave him everything he needed for his paintings.

After several minutes resting he continued on his way meandering back along the canals. Crossing Keizersgracht and turning into Nieuwe Spiegelstraat, he stopped to look in the window of Kramer Antiek. This shop had a large collection of Delft ceramics and other interesting antiques for sale. He always had a look as he went past to see if there was anything new that he might be tempted to add to his collection.

He soon reached the end of Spiegelstraat and crossed Singlegracht to the front of the Rijksmuseum. He walked around the grand 19th century building to Museumplein, past the Van Gough and Stedelijk museums to Van Baerlestraat and continued to Ceintuurbaan. Soon the road took him into Sarphatipark and out the other end to cross Van Woustraat.

He decided to visit his wife just a few blocks away.

'Hello darling, how has your day been?' he said to Elke.

'I have had a nice day Peter,' she replied. 'On Friday you have the dealers from Antwerp and Brussels visiting during the day and my party in the evening, don't forget.'

'Oh no, another day wasted!' Peter lamented.

'It will not be a waste of time darlink. I hope the dealers will want to take several paintings.'

'Yes, but I will have to talk, and be nice to them and everyone at the party. It takes up so much time and energy.'

'Oh, you'll survive. Then next week I'm going to Paris to see the dealers there. I'll be gone for a week,' she said.

His wife had been looking after his business affairs for many years. When he first gained some fame, he left the business of selling his work to his dealer in London. But when he met Elke a few years later she insisted, 'Peter, you are being undersold and underpaid. You have to take control of your career and business.'

Elke came from a family of art and antique dealers in Holland, so he put her in charge of his affairs. She placed his paintings with several important art dealers across Europe and many for sold for higher prices that he had achieved in London. Fortunately, unlike some artists, he had always been prolific churning out paintings weekly or monthly at worst. Most years he had completed around thirty saleable works and apart from a few dips in output when they had children he had kept up the pace for many years.

Elke had done such a good job of representing him that when she suggested that they move from London to her home town of Amsterdam he agreed without hesitation.

'You will be closer to the European markets, and you will be inspired,' she said.

She was right on both counts. His figure paintings, landscapes and still lifes were more popular in France and Germany than they were in England or the USA. The Europeans liked his more impressionist style. In England they wanted shocking or outlandish abstract art. But his portraits were popular there as at that time he painted personalities from the London arts and film scene.

He felt at home in Amsterdam, as if he was always meant to be there. The only connection to England that still tugged at his heart was the girl he left behind. But it was she that left him, and he had no idea where she was now, or if she was even still alive.

Elke made him a cup of coffee and they chatted for a while.

'I'm going to go back to the studio now and work on my landscape.'

'Have you pulled out the paintings for the dealers to see on Friday?'

'No, I have no idea which paintings they will like my love.'

'Of course you don't, that's my job. I will come over at about 11 on Friday morning and arrange everything. The Van Stoep's will arrive at 12. See you then schatse.'

They kissed goodbye and the painter returned to his studio and worked until late in the evening on his painting.

2

The next morning the painter sat down in front of his easel as he did every day. He held his brush lightly in his hand and swished the clean bristles around in the palm of his free hand. He looked at the blank white canvas in front of him and slowly an image appeared to him, filling in the space until it was bursting with colour and vivid images in his mind. Then he set to work mixing burnt umber colour with linseed oil in perpetration to apply his first dark colour.

The door bell chimed, ding dong. He glanced at the clock, 10 am. He had agreed to help a new teacher from the art school. The head of the school had asked if he would meet the man, show him his studio and how he worked. The painter had worked with several of the art school employees over the years. Although he had never been an a teacher himself, he sometimes gave guest lectures. They called him master. He liked the respect the name implied, but he knew he didn't deserve to be called master, like Rembrandt.

He opened the door and saw a tall handsome fellow with dark curly hair and a trimmed beard. He looked young and earnest. 'Hello Gregor,' he said as he stood aside and beckoned the young man to enter.

'Thank you Master for agreeing to see me.'

'Of course, anything for the school. I'm only too happy to impart some of my knowledge, and Professor Van Damme assures me that you are very talented.'

Gregor walked in and looked around the room. Paintings were hung on all four walls from to the top of the high ceilinged studio to near the level of the wooden floor three or four deep. A large set of windows took up half of the space on one wall and looked out onto the communal gardens with many trees and houses on the other side.

A table was placed In the middle of the room covered in jars filled with paint brushes and tubes of oil paint some new, many squeezed to near empty. A tall easel stood next to the table with a large blank canvas held in its grips. In front of it was a stool.

The room smelled of linseed oil and turpentine and the pallid morning light made soft edges and left many dark spaces in the corners of the large open space.

'I see you are about to begin a painting Master, forgive me for intruding.'

'You are not intruding, I was just musing in front of the canvas trying to decide what to paint, and call me Peter, please.'

'So you haven't yet decided what you are going to paint.'

'I never do. Every morning I try to start a new painting. I have many half conceived ideas in my head. Sometime inspiration comes, and sometimes not. If my mind stays blank for too long I go back to one of my many uncompleted projects.'

Gregor slowly walked around the room examining the paintings. There were indeed many works in progress lining the walls with yet more stacked on the floor leaning against the walls. There were still lives with flowers and fruit, pastoral scenes, moody interiors with shadowy figures, abstract splashes of colour, cubist explosions, and nudes, both male and female.

'Peter, you do have a lot of paintings on the go, and so many different styles and subjects.'

'Well Gregor, if you want to paint for a living, to be an artist, you have to be proficient in all styles of painting. Today you may say, 'I will paint a Rembrandt portrait', the next, an early Picasso. No matter what the style or subject you must be able to accomplish it.

'However, eventually, you must confront the real problem that every would-be artist faces, their existential crisis, what do *I* want to paint? What do *I* have to say?'

'What is it that you want to paint Peter?'

'Life,' he answered. 'A life, all of life, life from beginning to end. I want to transcend time and paint the whole sum of a person. I want the viewer to see every experience that the subject endured and let their true nature shine out through it all. One year or one thousand years, every sigh and blow, every emotion and experience. So that the viewer can see the entire story and understand, touch the true nature of my subject which could be a cup, an apple or a person.'

'You have succeeded many times over. Your prolific work is world famous.'

'No no, I have failed miserably. I have never succeeded in achieving that. This failure tears at my heart. I long for success. But now, I am old, and I fear I will never reach my goal.'

'You aren't that old. Have heart and never give in. But you must have come close at least?'

'Once I did, an old subject. It was a painting of a woman, a girl. But the painting is lost. It pains me too much to even remember it.'

'It is a shame that you no longer have the painting. But now time has passed and you are a more complete artist. Perhaps you can recreate it and finally achieve your goal.'

'It's not so simple Gregor. I have to have the vision, feel the passion. What I had, I lost. It was my own fault of course. No, I don't think I can ever get back that feeling of completeness. The sense of oneness with my subject, the girl I loved.'

'So she was your first love, the one that broke your heart? I can see that the cut was deep. But you are married and your love of your wife is famous.'

'Ah, you come too close. I can't express myself very well in words. This is why I am a painter, my expression is visual. Ignore what I just said, it was mere meanderings.'

The conversation awakened his memory, and now after many years of hiding it away in the deepest recesses of his heart, the door creaked open and the memory of her musky scent awakened his senses. His mind was now filled with her movements, her laugh, glinting eyes and luscious hair. He felt as if he could touch her after crossing an ocean of time. His first love filled his vision. But now, as then, all those years ago, the vision faded, she was gone and he was alone once more.

Gregor asked, 'You don't do many portraits nowadays do you? There are many famous portraits in your early work.'

'No I haven't painted portraits for years.'

'What about figure paintings, nudes?'

'No, I no longer do figure painting either.'

'So you don't use models any longer?'

'No, Gregor, as I said, I want to paint the essence of my subjects. To do that for a real live person is emotionally and physically draining. I need to feel so much empathy with the sitter I must become them. No, it is too difficult for me now.

'Instead I paint from my memory, my imagination. That way I only have to take on the persona of the image in my mind, not a real living and breathing creature. Just a two dimensional image. So if I paint a woman, she can be dancing, or gazing, or loving. But she is not alive. When I put the brush down, I can leave her on the canvas. With a live sitter the character haunts me day and night.'

'Maybe if you found the right sitter you could finish the masterpiece you long to create.'

'No no, Gregor, now I only want to paint the visions that come to me from everyday life. The scenes I see played out around me here in Amsterdam. But all this talk of art has exhausted me. I must rest now, please leave.'

'I will leave you now of course, but may I return?'

'Yes yes come another day.'

'I have a friend I would like to bring along. She would love to see your studio.'

'Yes Gregor, bring her along why not,' he said ushering him out the door.

He sat in front of his blank canvas again. The vision he had glimpsed of his new work had vanished from his mind's eye. He sat for as long as he could bear then gave up. 'Ah, it's gone, my day is ruined!'

He decided to go for a walk instead. He slammed the door to his studio and creaked down the narrow and steep staircase and opened the front door. He squeezed past rows of parked bicycles and walked down Govert Flinckstraat, through Albert Cuypmarkt to Sarphati Park to feed the ducks on the pond.

He sat on a bench and threw crumbs in the water. Swallows flew aerobatics over the pond chasing insects. He picked out one swallow and locked his eyes onto it following it as it flew up then banked hard left swooping around in a graceful arc and pulling up to a stall to catch an insect then plunging down again to pick up speed pulling straight just above the water of the pond and whirling around to the right.

He loved to watch birds, and he could paint them in any pose, resting or flying. He had it all captured in his head.

His meeting with Gregor had disturbed him. It had awakened his memory of the lost painting of his lost lover. He had nearly captured her essence in the painting and was close to completing it. But then there was that night, and she was gone. When he finally accepted that she was never going to return to him, he destroyed the painting in tears and torment, but that was so many years ago.

After a while he grew weary of watching the birds and returned to the studio. He worked on his paintings as best as he could for the rest of the week. After a few days he managed to drive Gregor and his lost masterpiece from his mind.

3

On Friday morning the painter's wife breezed into the studio. She was wearing a kaftan and a long silk scarf that wafted out behind her as she strode into the studio.

'Goedemorgen schatse, have you finished any more paintings?' she asked.

'No Elke, just more ideas and half finished works.'

'Well no problem, I will pull out a selection for the dealers.'

She rummagged through the paintings stacked on the ground and separated out out paintings that she thought would sell.

'Ah, this one yes. Oh schatse, I had forgotten abou this one! Why has this not bee sold before now? It will walk out the door. This one, no. I think I will take this away and put it in a cupboard somewhere, it's awful.'

'What do you mean Elke? I love that painting, leave it be.'

'Oh no, Peter, it should be hidden away. You can put it in your bed closet if you like. But this one, yes, this was completed this year. I will put it on the easel and it can be the showpiece for our salon today.'

She picked up the large painting of a street scene of Amsterdam. There were trees along a canal and elegant waterfront buildings with cyclists moving back and forth. Birds flew through the air and Van Gough like clouds filled the sky.

'Yes darlink, this painting will sell to the boys from Antwerp for sure. Now let me see. What else have we got. This one, yes, how exciting!'

'No Elke, not that one, I can never sell that one, give it to me!'

Peter grabbed the painting from Elke, but she refused to let go of it. They wrestled with the painting bending the frame and pushing their elbows and foreheads into the canvas.

'Stop schatse, you're damaging the painting.'

Finally Elke managed to wrest the painting from Peter who slumped into a chair.

'It's not finished in any case,' he said.

Elke put it against the wall and stood back to regard it.

'Of course it's finished. If it wasn't for me you would never say a painting is finished. You would continue working on them for ever and a day.'

'You're right darling, none of my painting are up to scratch,' said Peter shaking his head in despair.

'Schatse, don't be sad.'

Elke crouched down and cupped the painter's face in her hands and kissed him on the forehead.

'Come now, your work is wonderful, people are moved by your paintings. More importantly your paintings move out the door. They sell fast. What better confirmation of your worth and talent could there be? Cheer up my dear, the Belgians will be here soon.'

She continued rummaging and looking at the paintings that were hung on the wall. She placed the paintings she had chosen strategically around the studio. Turning her attention to the state of the room she tidied things away, hiding sweaters and socks under the cushions on the sofa. She opened the windows to let some air in and washed his dishes and coffee cups that were placed empty and stained all around the studio.

Finally satisfied, she sat down on the sofa and took out a handkerchief to wipe her brow.

'Oh I'm exhausted now,' she proclaimed. 'I had better go and make myself beautiful.'

She went to the bathroom to touch up her make up and comb her hair. She re-emerged with a beaming smile on her face and threw her scarf over her shoulder dramatically.

'Now I'm ready to receive our guests.'

She looked ruefully at her husband. 'Go change your clothes. You look like a rag-a-muffin.'

Peter dutifully went to his bed closet and opened the big drawer below the bed and puled out a clean shirt and trousers. He changed his shoes, putting on an elegant pair of two toned loafers. He put a red cravat around his neck and tied a knot that he pushed to one side. He took his beret off the hatstand by the door and looking in the mirror placed it on his head, cocked it to one side and pulled it down.

'There, how's that?'

'You look so handsome darlink, oh, as beautiful as the day we met.'

The doorbell chimed, ding dong and Elke went to open the door. Speaking in Dutch she ushered two thin men dressed in black suits and wearing horn rimmed glasses into the studio.

'Peter, you remember the Van Der Stoep brothers, Baaf and Edgardo,' she said smiling while waving her hands in a flourish.

'Yes, yes of course I remember Baaf and Edgardo. How are you both? You look so well.'

The identical twins bowed their heads in unison. One of them, Peter felt sure it was Baaf, started speaking in a dialect that Peter could not understand at all. Baaf nodded his head towards Edgardo who took up where Baaf left off. Peter, totally confused, smiled and nodded his head enthusiastically.

Elke put her arm around Baaf's shoulder and whispering to him in Dutch guided him and Edgardo towards the paintings she had put on display. She pointed to one and stood back as if in awe at the beauty of the work.

The two men from Antwerp rubbed their thin boney chins and murmured to each other. They nodded to indicate that they had concluded their deliberations and continued to the next painting.

Elke walked them around the room and they spent several minutes examining each of the works. Fianally she brought them to the showcase painting on the easel.

The brothers stood back and rubbed their chins for an exceptionally long time. Eventually, Edgardo looked at Peter.

'Master, do you still paint portraits?' he asked in English.

'Portraits? No, I haven't painted a portrait for many years. Why are you interested in portraits now?'

'Baaf raised his finger to show that he would be the one to respond. There is a renewed interest in portraits. We are always asked about them but so few artists are painting them. Your portraits are wonderful, they have been your finest work over the years. They still trade for the highest prices of any of your works. Indeed Peter, if it wasn't for your fame as a portrait artist your other works would attract lower prices.'

Edgardo continued, 'I think telephones are the reason people want portraits.'

'Telephones?' said Elke puzzled.

'Yes Elke, telephones,' said Baaf.

'I think it is the new cultural importance of the selfie that has gripped the artistic subconciousness,' said Edgardo.

Baaf continued, 'Everyone is taking selfies. They think that this is art, and when they come into our gallery they are surprised there are so few smiling faces beaming out at them from the canvases. That after all, is what they see all around them in normal life.'

'Slefies? You must be insane. I am an artist, I don't do happy snaps for imbecile tourists! How about cats? Would you like me to paint cats also?'

In unison Baaf and Edgardo smilled, raised their index fingers, nodded enthusiastically and said, 'Cats! Yes please, we can sell as many pictures of cats as you can supply us.'

A short while later, after Elke had shown the brothers from Antwerp out the door, the painter and his wife slumped down into the sofa.

'Schatse, I'm sorry. The brothers have sold so many of your painting in the past. I had no idea they were going so down market now. They say the market has changed, and they need to find new types of material to sell.'

'Never mind my darling, as long as you don't want me to start painting selfies,' said Peter.

'Although they are right of course. Your most famous paintings are your portraits. But no matter, in a few minutes Monsieur Dupont from Brussels will be arriving. We shall see what's in fashion for paintings in the Belgian capital. He sells mostly to EU diplomats and politicians. A totally different market.'

The painter and his wife had moved from London to Amsterdam thirty years ago. But Peter had struggled to learn Dutch. Part of the problem was that Dutch people invariably spoke better English than he could ever hope to speak Dutch. So they usually replied to his falting destruction of their language in English, and the conversation continued that way.

The other problem was that people from different regions in Holland and Flemish Belgium spoke different dialects. They did not just sound different but used different words and idioms. Dutch people could move between the dialects without difficulty. But outsiders were soon left behind.

A short while later the doorbell rang again and Elke showed French speaking Marcel Dupont into the studio.

'Hello Marcel, so nice to see you again,' said Peter.

'Always a pleasure to see what you have been working on my dear Peter,' said Marcel smiling and shaking Peter's hand.

'Come, let me show you his latest oeuvre,' said Elke. She took Marcel directly to the showcase painting on the easle.

'I love it,' he said. 'Of course I must have this one. It will quickly sell I am sure.'

'So you don't want me to do portraits?' Asked Peter.

'If you would like to come to Brussels and paint EU bureaucrats and politicians I am sure you could make a market. But the people I sell to aren't interested in anybody else's image. They only want to see themselves, on TV, the internet. Or they want their illustrious portrait added to a staircase or conference room somewhere in the EU buildings.

'But this painting of Amsterdam will be popular. They can take it back to their offices in Poland or Slovenia and they will seem like cultured world travellers.'

Marcel said he would take the Amsterdam scene and four other paintings on consignment. After pleasantries he got up to leave. Muoi, muoi, Elke kissed him on both cheeks, 'So nice to see you Marcel. The paintings will be ready for shipment as soon as possible.'

Pleased with their days work, Elke and Peter hugged as they said goodbye. 'You won't forget to come to my soirée?' asked Elke.

'No, of course not darling, I'll see you this evening,' said Peter.

After their children had grown up and left home, the two of them had agreed that Peter would live in the studio and Elke would stay in their family home. Elke liked to entertain, staging elaborate parties. During the day her friends would drop by the apartment and have a chat while drinking coffee and eating cake. She was involved in several charities and was on the councils of several art institutions across Holland.

Peter had become more reclusive and shied away from all the noise and people that Elke loved. He began to spend some nights sleeping at the studio, and eventually moved in full time.

This evening she had arranged an informal drinks and canapés affair. He had no idea who would be there and cared not. But he would go along for a while to keep his wife happy

Now he was alone again and he placed his blank canvas back on the easel.

4

As the twilight light changed to a dreamy summer mood the painter put down his paint brush and changed his clothes for his wife's soirée. He put on his red cravat and pulled his beret over to the left, just so. I must get into character, he thought.

He climbed the narrow stairs to the top floor apartment. The door was open and as he approached he heard laughter and glasses clinking.

Elke was in the far corner of the living room talking to a group of people, waving her arms in the air in a dramatic way. She was wearing a gold coloured kaftan and turban. The apartment was filled with people.

Peter went into his old study to escape the crowd, but there were several people in there already. He was about to leave when Professor Van Damme said, 'Dear Peter how are you,' his beaming face close to his.

'Van Damme, sorry I didn't see you there, I'm fine thanks. I met that fellow from the school you wanted me to see, Gregor.'

'Yes, you did indeed and he is here tonight, let me see, oh there he is, come and say hello.'

Van Damme lead Peter back into the living room to where Gregor was standing by a window.

'Peter, good to see you again.' said Gregor. 'Let me introduce you to my fiance, Elenore.'

A graceful young woman standing next to Gregor raised her hand for him to shake. Peter instinctively took it gently and kissed the back of her fingers.

'Delighted to meet you Elenore.'

She smiled and bowed her head slightly. Peter was struck by her smile and eyes. She looked so reminiscent, so much like the women he knew in his youth. She was full of life, charm, relaxed and confident.

'So Peter this is your family home?' said Gregor.

'Yes it is, but I spend most of my time at the studio nowadays.'

Van Damme and Gregor peppered Peter with questions about his life in Amsterdam and his children. They wanted to know more about his recent work. Peter answered as matter of factly as he could. He disliked chit chat. All the while he could not stop glancing at Elenore, her large brown eyes, full lips and elegant neck.

Van Damme and Gregor discussed the work in the student exhibition that was to be held soon. Peter nodded, but their voices merged into the noise of the party.

'Tell me Elenore, what to you do?' he said.

'I work at the Rijksmuseum in administration.'

'Are you an artist Elenore?' Peter asked.

'I draw a little,' she said.

'She does some life modelling at the school, people draw her,' Gregor piped in.

Peter looked up at Gregor and Van Damme. They had stopped talking, noticing the Peter was no longer listening to them.

'Gregor told me about your studio. I would love to see it sometime,' said Elenore.

Peter turned back to her, 'Why not this evening? It's only around the corner,' he said.

'Ah, thanks for the invite,' said Gregor, 'let's enjoy the party first.'

Van Damme raised his hand and said, 'Look, there is the Director of the Stedelijk, let me introduce these two to him.'

Peter nodded politely as Van Damme lead them away, weaving their way though the crowd to the other side of the room.

Peter squeezed between people talking and clinking their glasses until he was standing next to his wife.

Elke welcomed him into the centre of a circle of admiring people. Peter was the star attraction, as he always was at Elke's parties. She showed him off and he smiled politely.

Elke takes care of business, thank goodness, so I don't have to. All I have to do is play the master painter every now and then, he reminded himself.

'Oh darlink, you look so handsome. Let me introduce you to Louis who is a curator at the National Gallery in London.'

'Charmed to meet you Peter, I am a great admirer of your work. I hope we will see some new figure paintings from you soon,' said a smiling man bowing as he put out his hand for Peter to shake.

'Peter you remember Maestro Rodrigo from the Giovine Orchestra Genoa,' said Elke.

On it went, his evening on the red carpet, playing royalty to the upper echelons of the European art industry. At least the ones who happened to be in Amsterdam that week for what ever reason. None of them would miss Elke's soirée, unless there was something better on. But Elke was too canny to allow that to happen. Her parties were always perfectly timed so as not to clash with any other evening event, and she only held them when there was something happening in Amsterdam that would attract the right people.

The circle of people around Elke and Peter continually changed as guests were introduced to Peter, made a few sentences of polite conversation, until the circle turned once more, and the next person was introduced.

Peter was talking to the director of a Swiss museum when he noticed Elenore across the room. She was with Gregor who was holding forth talking insistently to some fellow. Elenore was pretending to be involved and interested. But Peter noticed, yes, she is, she's looking at me. He smiled at the Swiss gentleman and nodded, but he could not avert his eyes from Elenore.

The circle turned, and he was now introduced to a large woman with an even larger hat. She was, 'Sooo delighted to meet the great master,' she said in an exaggerated posh English accent.

Peter looked again towards Elenore and she was looking straight at him. I am the centre of attention, of course she's looking at me. Nothing more to read into that, he thought. But he felt an attraction to her that he had not felt towards any woman for as long as he could remember.

He turned his back to Elenore, and the circle of people, including Elke, shuffled their feet and rearranged the circle to a new orientation around the painter.

Peter endured as long as he could. Eventually, he caught Elke's eye, and she understood. 'Oh darlink, you have been so gracious this evening. You can go whenever is suits you dear. I'll come over and see you before I leave for Paris,' she whispered into his ear.

Peter waited for Elke to start speaking in a loud voice to the circle of people in general about some topic of the day. That was his queue that he could shuffle away while the audience was distracted.

As he reached the front hallway on his way out he passed Elenore and Gregor who was talking with great passion to some poor man whose bored eyes were transfixed on Gregor's convulsed face.

'Peter, are you leaving?' said Elenore, touching his elbow.

'Yes, parties are not for me.'

'What about the tour of your studio?'

'Come over in a little while if you like. Don't leave it too late.'

'I would like to. I will drag Gregor away soon if I can.'

As he walked down Van Woustraat Peter took off his beret and cravat and stuffed them in his pocket. He soon arrived at the studio, and after only a short while the doorbell chimed.

He opened the door, 'Come in, you are both welcome,' he said.

'Thank you Peter, may we look around?' said Gregor.

'Yes of course.'

The couple paced along the walls of the studio regarding the many artworks.

'This is a very interesting work,' said Gregor pointing to a pastel drawing of a female nude high up on the wall.'

'That was just an exercise, a study that I did some years ago.'

'Do you still paint from live models? Asked Elenore'

'No, not for years. I have no time or need for models any longer. I paint from the visions I have in my head.'

Elenore smiled at him and continued to stroll along the row of paintings. She was not tall but slender. Her face was a perfect shape for her well proportioned body.

'I've seen many photos of your paintings,' said Elenore.

Gregor said, 'She was interested to see some of your work up close, and your studio. She was impressed that I had met you.'

'Well I hope you enjoy my works. The best ones aren't in the studio of course. They've been sold. Still there are a few on display here that I am happy with,' said Peter.

'They are very good,' said Elenore. 'I like your city scenes, but there are no portraits here.'

'Why does everyone go on about my portraits? I have told everyone, I do not do portraits anymore.'

'Your figure paintings are my favourites, though,' she said.

'Peter, maybe it's time that you painted from life again, so you can complete your work, recreate your masterpiece,' said Gregor.

Peter was puzzled by this intrusion, people pushing him to paint portraits and nudes that he didn't want to paint anymore. 'Did Professor Van Damme put you up to this?' demanded Peter.

'No, not at all Peter. Rather, when I found out that you were connected to the school and the Professor said I could meet you, it was your figure paintings that I thought of. Then you told me that you had never completed your masterpiece. I, we, would like to help you. That is all, just some encouragement from admirers.'

Until Peter had met Elenore he was sure that he would never use a model again. But he now looked at her in a new light. She had bright shining eyes. Her face was beautiful. But he could not see her figure under her loose clothes.

'You say you would like to help me?'

'Yes, if we can,' said Gregor.

'Elenore does life modelling? She could sit for me. Perhaps that will encourage me to try once more,' said Peter

Elenore's eyes drooped to the floor and she swished around and walked back up the line of paintings. She looked at Gregor. He smiled back at her. 'I don't mind chéri. Why not?' he said.

Elenore turned to look at the painter, 'I'll do it, if you're sure you want me to,' she said.

'I think so, but show me,' said Peter, 'I need to see what you look like.'

Elenore's face retreated, she looked taken aback. 'What, right now?'

'Yes yes, let's have a look. I have no time to waste my dear.'

She looked around the room for some where to disrobe.

'Over there,' Peter pointed to Chinese blinds in a corner of the studio. They had been used by his models in the past.

Elenore went behind them and one by one her garments were draped over the divider. Soon she emerged, naked, and stood in the middle of the room. She did several quick poses, as models do at the start of a life drawing class. Then she stopped and stood silently before Peter.

Her body was beautiful. She had a perfect figure with a thin waist with well proportioned behind and thighs. Her breasts were firm but soft and welcoming.

'Please, turn around.' he said.

She slowly turned a full circle with her arms outstretched.

'Alright, I will paint you. I would like to start as soon as possible, when can you come?'

'It depends, how many sittings do you think you will need?' asked Elenore.

'As many as it takes. I told Gregor, I don't paint in half measures. It is all or nothing for me. I will continue until I finish. I will pay the standard modelling fee of course.'

Elenore put her clothes back on and stood whispering to Gregor. After a few minutes Gregor said, 'She will come tomorrow if you like.'

'Tomorrow it is at 10 am, sharp,' said Peter.

He showed them out giving nothing more of his emotions away. They seemed a little unsure of themselves as they departed. Peter hadn't though they would agree so easily. But it was all Gregor's fault, his suggestion.

Peter had early success painting celebrity portraits. That's why they think my portraits are the best. It is because the sitters are famous, not because the paintings are good, he thought.

Sevdral of his portraits had been purchased by museums, and they brought him fame. But they were not his best paintings at all, in his opinion. I painted some famous people. Big deal, the paintings are in museums, ridiculous.

Far from considering them, '*his most important contributions to contemporary art*', as one famous Australian art critic described them, he thought they were actually terrible.

He considered some of his life paintings, nudes, to be very good and they also sold well. He was happy about their success.

Some people have taste, understand the meaning of human expression, he mused.

In his mind, the best work he ever created was of his lover Lana whom he painted at the beginning of his career, soon after graduating from Goldsmiths College, so long ago.

Ah, Lana, what a beautiful girl, what memories, what a painting. It was the closest I have ever come to creating a painting that lived by itself, something alive and real, he lamented.

Peter was interested in depicting the human condition as vulnerable, tender, transcendent and sublime. He had no wish to paint heroes, or fallen angels, but living humans, true to their inherent nature.

But after Lana left him that night, no, he could never get back to that paradise lost. He flet abandoned, in a struggle for survival, searching for meaning. He was lost in a confusion of broken images and pain, until he met Elke. She consoled him, and brought him understand that life is to be lived. 'Heaven can wait, at least a little while,' she said.

But now, yes, he could see in Elenore the elements he needed to make his perfect painting, the essence of his lover. He felt he could achieve the same completeness that he had accomplished with his original work.

There was something about her erotic persona that stirred him the same way as Lana. She had the same fire in her eyes. He was intrigued by her. The painter determined to try once more, to strive for perfection. He was now filled with excitement and could barley wait to embark on his new project.

5

Peter slept lightly that night he was so excited. He woke early as usual and made his breakfast.

He then prepared a few props around the studio for his model to use. His models stand had been neglected for a long time and was in a corner with a bookshelf on it. He pulled it to the centre of the room and dusted it off. He Dragged the sofa to the side of the stand at an angle to the windows so as to catch the morning light and arranged chairs in various positions.

Rummaging in his art supply cabinet he pulled out one large and one small drawing pad. He made sure he had a good supply of charcoals, pastels and a sheaf of loose paper ready on his table.

Waiting for what seemed like eternity, at 10 am sharp, ding dong, the doorbell chimed and he rushed to the door.

'Good morning Elenore, please come in.'

Elenore's eyes fixed on his, with a faint smile she proceeded without talking to the Chinese blinds and disrobed.

The painter waved his hand at towards the stand and she took her place.

'I would like you to make a series of gestures and then hold the pose for one minute please,' he said.

She stretched her arms out forward as in a ballet move and bent her knees in a soft plié.

After a minute the painter said, 'New pose.'

She hesitated, then moved. This time she put her hands on her hips and twisted her torso to the right keeping her legs firm and straight.

Peter sat on his stool and drew her gestures on his small pad, quickly with a square piece of charcoal. Morning light streamed diagonally through the windows illuminating her body highlighting her contours and her shape. He only made quick outlines of her as if feeling out the limits of her body, it's size and proportions.

After ten poses, he said, 'You can rest now.'

Without speaking she returned to the Chinese blinds and put on a robe that she had brought with her.

'Would you like some fruit?' said Peter gesturing towards a bowl in the kitchen.'

'Yes thank you,' said Elenore picking up an apple.

She took a bite and walked to the sofa and sat down. After a few minutes, Peter said, 'New pose, this time five minutes.'

Elenore unwrapped her robe, leaving it behind her on the sofa and resumed her position on the stand. She made a new gesture, still standing.

Peter continued to draw with his charcoal this time making thicker smudged lines, feeling out her form and weight.

'New pose, but sit now. You won't be able to hold many poses for five minutes if you are standing. Do something different,' said Peter.

She sat down, and her gestures became more exaggerated. She folded her body over like Rodin's La Danaid. The next pose she arched backwards, her arms outstretched and hands propped on the sofa supporting her weight with her breasts thrust upwards.

Peter drew her, searching for her inner impulse, the motivation that precipitated each gesture that ended in the pose that resulted.

She held six poses, then once again, Peter said, 'You may rest now.'

She put on her robe, laid back on the sofa and closed her eyes.

'Very good Elenore, you are an excellent model. Take ten minutes to rest.'

'Thank you master,' said Elenore.

'Master?' Peter chuckled. 'You are not my servant. I am your servant, your admirer.'

Peter put his small pad down and cast his fingers across his box of pastels rolling them as if along piano keys. He chose one and placed it on his large drawing pad in preparation.

After a while Elenore opened her eyes and glanced a the clock on the wall. Ten minutes had passed and shes asked, 'Do you wish a longer pose this time?'

'Yes, stay where you are on the sofa.'

She slipped off her robe and lying on her side curled up her legs and rested her head on her hand with her elbow on the sofa and yawned.

Peter moved his stool in front of the window to see her with the light shining directly on her and began to draw.

He drew shapes, the lines of arms, legs, the curve of her muscles and belly. He wasn't interested in her, the woman, only in capturing her form. But he knew this would soon change. To make an interesting painting he needed more than an elegant or beautiful gesture or body. He needed the seek out the uniqueness of his model, her inner self.

At least this was his idea, his desire. Other figure painters had different approaches. He had studied the greats of course at college and all his life, Leonardo, Rembrandt.

'Picasso, the greatest portraitist of all time,' he mumbled to himself.

'What was that about Picasso Peter?'

'I was just saying to my self, he was able to capture something immortal, the essence of humanity. Picasso didn't use models, at least not after his younger years. He painted and drew from his memory. But he knew the people he was depicting. He would always be drawing while he was talking, eating, drinking. He observed everyone, their gestures, the way they moved. He spent much time with the people he depicted, the women in his life, especially his lovers, his wives.'

'So are you are going to paint me with three heads and bulging eyes?' Asked Elenore.

'No, it was Picasso's early portraits that I am referring to.

'You said that you hadn't used models for a long time. Why do you want me now?'

'Because Gregor, Van Damme, yourself, everyone seems to want me to paint a real person again. I have tried before to achieve some perfection, but I failed. This time, with you, perhaps I will succeed.

'Other artists use a model for a few sessions to obtain what they need. For a long time I have preferred to paint only from memory and reference drawings I have made. But I see now that those works have been lifeless. My landscapes and still lives have been popular because they seem genuine to the viewers. But my paintings of people have, at least in my mind, missed the mark, failures, which is why I gave up. With you I feel I have another chance to succeed, to paint a human being again.'

'How many sessions will you need me for?'

'I don't know Elenore. This painting is different. I am trying to go back to what I had once achieved, or nearly. I want to capture you, on canvas that is.'

Elenore felt sleepy, relaxed. She had been trepidatious about modelling for the painter. Gregor had encouraged her, 'He's a famous painter, it will do you good, give you notoriety to be his muse,' he said.

I don't need notoriety, she thought, but she was intrigued by Peter. Now having agreed to come and pose for him, she felt as if it was natural. She felt shielded and happy under his gaze.

Then the painter said, 'New pose.'

She glanced at the clock, and 15 minutes had elapsed. She sat up put her feet on the floor and stretched her arms.

Peter said, 'I want something different this time. Here, allow me.' He gently put his hand on her ankle and lifted her leg up and onto the sofa and raising her knee, 'Lie backwards,' he said.

She stretched back with her head on a cushion and went to lift her other leg onto the sofa but Peter said, 'No, leave your foot where it is.'

He placed a chair straight in front of her and sat down, looking at her prone body with her legs spread. He picked up his pad and began to draw.

For the first time Elenore felt uneasy, compromised.

'Don't worry Elenore. I am just trying a pose. I don't know if it will be what ultimately reveals you to me, but I must look at you in every way.' Peter smiled, 'I'm not so interested in your anatomy. I want to free you from your inhibitions. I must know you intimately. There can be no holding back.'

He drew fast making scraping sounds with the pastel. After some time he said, 'New pose, please turn sideways.'

He stood up and touched her ankle, gently he hooked her leg over the arm of the sofa, picked up her hands and folded them across her belly.

Continuing to draw quickly, his eyes never seemed to leave her to check what he had drawn. He had a slight smile on his face, but seemed lost in concentration.

Peter continued to talk to her while he drew. 'You are right about Picasso of course. At the beginning of the 20th century, our conceptions of art were thrown up in the air. When they landed, we had Fauvism, Expressionism, Cubism, Dada and Surrealism. Artists painted people from their dreams, subconscious and divorced them entirely from what they actually looked like.

'I'm not interested in the surrealist dream image, stylised or exploded. But the true nature of the model, what ever that might be, and I have to find that out about you.'

After this pose Peter looked at the clock and said, 'Time's up, that's it for today.'

It was 12 noon and Elenore put on her clothes.

The next day at 10 am Elenore arrived again at the studio. She disrobed and stood feet apart her arms by her side on the stand. 'What would you like today?'

Peter looked at her and swished a paint brush around in his hand. His eyes followed the contours of her face and ear. He looked at every detail as his eyes continued down her gentle neck to her clavicle, down her arm, breasts and abdomen to her pelvic region and pubis.

Peter knew that to make his painting special, a masterpiece, he needed to come so close to his model, Elenore, that he was inside her skin, and therein was the peril for them both.

'I need more from you. Yesterday you were flat, emotionless. I need to see some tension, something defiant expressive. I know what your body looks like. I can see how you move, your proportions. You are graceful, but now I need something more dynamic.'

Elenore was puzzled. She had posed for drawing classes at the art school many times. She was used to eyes regarding her, seeing her body. But the students were all lifeless. They never spoke or asked anything of her. She just made a gesture and held a pose.

She stepped off the stand and walked around the room, looking at the paintings on the walls. She raised her arms and swung around. She danced around the room turning in circles, while Peter looked at her, his eyes, squinting, critical.

Then she stopped and looked him in the eyes. He stood up and went to her and ran his hands across the skin of her arms and shoulders and back. Dropping to his knees, his hands pressed across her belly and down her behind, squeezing her muscles, caressing her thighs as if feeling a sculpture. He breathed in her scent as his face came close to her body. His lips gently kissed the back of her knee.

'Yes, I need to feel you, drink you in, not just with my eyes, but with all my senses.'

He stood back and went to hes easel. He had pinned a sheet of paper to a large board. Picking up a compressed charcoal stick he began to draw. Soon he pulled the sheet off the easel and replaced it with another.

'New pose, do something more expressive, let me inside of you.'

Elenore tried several poses, each more tormented. Peter drew for several minutes then said 'new pose,' and she tried once more.

This time she lay back on the sofa, leaning on one elbow, her legs apart draped over the edge, her pelvis twisted and sex exposed.

'I like this one,' said Peter

She felt the caress of his eyes, and her skin tingled. She looked at his thin figure, bony hands that seemed so delft, skilled. His movements were quick, his hand moving over the paper and the charcoal making scratching noises. His eyes were fixed on her. She could still feel his hands on her, gentle but insistent.

She smiled, and Peter said, 'What are yo looking so happy about?'

A little laugh came out of her and she covered her mouth with her hand. 'I don't know, I'm relaxing I suppose.'

Peter put his charcoal down and said, 'Yes well, you can relax now. That will do for today.'

'Oh so soon.' Elenore looked at the clock, it was 12 noon. She felt a slight disappointment that the session was over, and she hesitated while putting her clothes back on.

'Would you like a coffee?' asked Peter.

'Yes, thanks.'

Peter made a jug of filter coffee, and they sat down at the kitchen counter together.

'Tell me about Gregor,' said Peter.

'Oh, well, he's my lover, my fiance. We live together.'

'When will you be married?'

'There is no date set yet. He wants to secure his career before making the final commitment.'

'So you are only slightly engaged?' said Peter.

Elenore blushed and looked the painter in the eyes. 'Yes, just a little bit.'

As she was leaving, he went with her to the door. He put his hand over her shoulder to reach the handle. She turned around and looked up into his face her lips parted, her eyes sought out his. They kissed, softly.

'You are so beautiful my dear,' he said.

'Peter, I don't know, but you make me feel special.' She said turning back to the closed door.

Peter turned the handle and pulled the door open. She glanced back at him, her eyes flashing. Then ran down the stairs.

As she walked home her heart pulsed and she felt a flush in her cheeks. Inwardly smiling, fondness for the painter filled her thoughts, like a young girl's crush. He's an eccentric old man, don't get carried away, she told herself.

At the end of the day Gregor came home from work. 'How did the session go today?' he asked.

'It went much better Gregor. I can see that Peter has an artistic idea in mind, and he seems to like the way it's going. He has a nice smile and soft hands.'

'Soft hands? Did he touch you?'

'Yes, he said he needed to experience my form with all his senses, not just sight. He needs to truly understand my physique and get beneath my skin.'

'Elenore, I'm no longer sure this is a good idea! I don't think you should go back again. This is getting out of hand, what have I gotten us into?'

'Gregor, don't be so silly. He just rubbed my shoulders, touched my hands. Besides, he's an old man.'

'Is that all he did? Well, that's perfectly alright then. Standing naked before him and he just rubbed your shoulders. What will he rub next time? Honestly darling I didn't think this through. You should just not go back again. I will go see him and tell him you are too busy for any more sittings.'

'You're a painter yourself, and you even teach life painting. Am I to suppose that you proposition your models?'

'Of course not. I'm a professional, and I don't see the woman, or man for that matter. I'm looking at form, shape, curves. There is nothing erotic about it.'

Elenore folded her arms, looked Gregor in the eye and said, 'It's a different experience being with a real artist, just me and him without a classroom full of students dutifully painting shapes and never moving.

He's trying to create something worthwhile, real art. I'm going back tomorrow whether you like it or not. He's a genius, and I want to see the finished work.'

In the early evening Elke left her apartment and walked over to the studio. 'How are you darlink, I came to see you as I'm off to Paris in the morning,' she said as she breezed in the door. 'What a great success my party was, everyone was there.'

Peter was surprised by her visit, and he closed his drawing pad and moved to hide his papers.

Elke looked around the studio and saw the models stand, the easel with a nude drawing on it, and the robe still draped over the Chinese blinds.

'You have a model, no, I don't believe it,' she said. 'Yes, I am going to try again, try to finish my painting.'

'Who is the model, where did you find her?'

'She's from the school, shes the lover of one of the teachers. It's your fault. I met her at your party.'

'Schatse, you don't want to go down this route. You know how sensitive you are. You're playing with fire,' she said.

'No Elke, I will be fine. It's just a painting. Everyone wants me to paint people again.'

'It's just a painting? It's never just a painting for you. Your works are like your children. You love them and never want to let them go. You try do dominate them, own them as if you could live your life in them. Now you want to paint a beautiful young woman? My God, you'll loose yourself Peter.'

'You didn't object to me painting nudes in the past. We made an agreement. I am the painter, and I have full creative control of my work. You are my manager.'

'That was years ago when you were in your prime. You're frail now, emotionally. I don't know where you'll end up. Besides, I leave for Paris tomorrow. You'll be all alone.'

'I forgot that you were going to Paris. When you're there you can sound the dealers out. Do they also wish I would return to figure painting?'

'Alright then, painter, master. I'll go to Paris for a week and sell your paintings for you. I hope you'll still be here when I get back and not have run away with your young model.'

After Elke left, he opened a bottle of wine for the first time in many months. The dry sparkling liquid bubbled down into his stomach and a happiness came over him. Yes, he could see her again, feel her in his heart. It was as if they had just met for the first time.

6

When Peter woke the next morning, his mood had changed. Last night he had fallen asleep with happy memories of Lana and how much she loved him. But now he remembered their separateness, the times when she was cold and uncaring. She would push him away, and he would be in turmoil until she relented and was tender to him once more. He felt betrayed by her. How could she treat him so when he loved her so much?

He tried to put these memories out of his mind and prepared the studio for Elenore. But he knew he needed some tension between him and his model. He could not simply paint a pretty picture and hope to create a masterpiece. He opened the door and waited for Elenore's arrival.

Elenore ran up the stairs, and went straight in.

'You seem happy today,' said Peter.

'I am enjoying our sessions. Would you like the same pose as yesterday?'

'No, I haven't found you yet. You must try harder.' He turned away from her and sat on his stool with a stern expression.

After the tenderness of the night before Elenore felt a wave of disappointment. Peter seems distant today, yesterday he seemed so close to me, she thought.

The memory of the sensation she felt as his eyes seemed to ravish her was still fresh. His hands so searching. She looked at his face as he pinned a new sheet of paper to the easel. He seemed so determined but distant. She was no longer sure of him.

Peter said, 'New pose.'

She sat on a chair and placed her chin on her hand.

'Charming,' Peter said and smiled.

After some minutes he again said, 'New pose.'

The morning progressed and Elenore tried many poses. Noon came and went, but today, Peter made no move to stop the session.

In the mid afternoon Peter said, 'Alright, we had better stop and eat something.'

He shook his head as he put his pastel down and walked over to the kitchen.

Elenore put on her robe on and followed him. He stood by the counter and took a loaf of bread out and began to hack off pieces with a knife. She stood close to him and put her hand on his shoulder. Her breast brushed against his arm.

'Are you disappointed in me today Peter?'

'No darling, It's me, I feel apart from you. Yesterday we were so close, but today, you seem as far away as ever. It's as though we are still separated by that ocean of time.'

Elenore tightened her fingers into his shoulder and pressed her body to his, 'We are together, let's be together,' she whispered.

Peter moved away from her and continued to prepare food for them, They ate in silence until peter said, 'New pose, I want you to reach out to me, give me everything, I need to posses you.'

Elenore pushed away from him, she felt scorned. 'You don't really want to know me. You just want to torment me.'

She struck a pose. Her face became twisted in anger. Peter drew quickly but soon demanded a new pose and another, new pose, new pose.

'You must give me more. You're hiding, reveal your self to me,' Peter demanded.

Exhausted, eventually neither the painter nor Elenore could do more. Elenore put her clothes on and looked at the painter. He looked away.

'Peter, I won't come tomorrow, you don't want me.'

'You can't abandon me, not again. We needed this tension today. Creating art is like giving birth, you have to push. It can be excruciating. But I promise you tomorrow we will make progress.'

'Today you were trying to hurt me, brush me aside,'

'I would never hurt you. I need you. This will be my masterpiece, my legacy. I promise tomorrow will be better. You will see.'

'Alright Peter, if I am here tomorrow we can continue. If I don't arrive at 10, you must let me be,' she said slamming the door and ran down the stairs.

Gregor was already home when she arrived. She did not tell him about the day, but he felt that something was wrong.

'I don't want you to see the painter again,' he said.

'You're right, I don't want to go any more.' she assured him.

'Was he cruel to you? Did he touch you? I'm going to go and see him right now!'

'No, no leave him be. The experience is just too intense for me. He's striving for something that can't be achieved. He wants some perfect being, something that I am not. I can't sit for him again, he's too demanding,' she said.

But the next morning Gregor went to work at the art school as usual. When it came time for her to go to the studio she found herself walking out the door.

She arrived on time, but today she was not happy and she slumped herself down on the sofa. She put one hand behind her head and the other on her lap. Her legs slightly bent and her torso turned towards Peter.

She felt rejected, and her eyes were filled with bitterness. But soon her face took on a defiant, independent glare. She tried to cover up her real feelings, but her lips trembled, beyond her control. A sad smile came across her face as her feelings turned to tenderness, a soft pain as if her lover had gone away.

Peter, watched as her face transfigured before him, telling a story that he read like a poem. He said, 'Keep that expression, keep it, don't move.'

He picked up his small pad and moved closer to her. He drew her face then tore the page from the pad, threw it behind him and started again. Several times he tore the page off the pad and started afresh. Eventually, he stopped and looked at what he had captured and smiled.

'What's the matter Peter? Can I move now?' she said

'What's the matter? Nothing at all. Yes, you can move, but remember that expression it was perfect.'

Elenore, felt relieved, after yesterday she wanted this to be the last session.

'I'm so happy Peter that at last you have got something. Is it enough, do you still need me?'

'Yes darling I still need you. But perhaps I have something I can work with now. Take up the pose from the other day again. Try to put that expression back on your face, but I have that at least, in my head and on paper. It is just how I remember you, that night.'

'What do you mean remember me?'

'Never mind, just take up that pose. But relax, this will take a while.

Elenore lay back on the sofa again and tried to remember her pose.

Peter moved about the studio quickly opening the drawers of a large plan chest. He rummaged through drawers of paper until he found what he wanted. He pulled out a large piece of thick paper and pinned it to the board on the easel.

He picked up a pastel and stood ready to draw. 'Come on, get the pose correct, and that expression, please, remember how you felt.'

Elenore bent her legs and twisted her torso. She tried to remember how bittersweet, insecure, and afraid she had felt but it was hard. Now that Peter was happy, so was she. Instead of spurned she felt delighted that they were making progress.

The two hours passed but Peter kept drawing. He glanced at the clock and said, 'You can't leave yet. Have a break, but today we must keep going until I have captured you.'

Peter continued drawing her in the same pose until late afternoon when he let her return home.

Pleased with his work he went to pour himself a glass of wine, but the bottle was empty. He put on his beret and picked up a bag and walked to the supermarket to buy more wine.

Peter had given up drinking some years ago. It seemed to distract him from his work, and he wanted nothing to get in his way. But now, he wanted to relax, to ponder his creation. He hadn't had feelings of this kind for so long. It was as if he was young again. The world seemed full of hope and promise and he dared to dream about the future.

'Yes my dear,' he said out loud, 'Now we are together again, nothing will make us part.'

He sat at his table transfixed by the image on his easel, sipping his wine he smiled, imagining the finished painting. In his mind he mixed every colour, painted every stroke. He realised that he would need more paint and a canvas, he decided to go to the artists supply shop first thing in the morning before the next session.

The next morning he put on his beret and walked over to the artist suppliers on Bilderdijkstraat. The door chime played it's off key melody as Peter walked into the empty shop.

This was the oldest and best artist suppliers in Amsterdam. The family run business had been in this location for generations. The cavernous store was filled with the finest paints, chalks, papers and top quality canvases. Peter had spent many happy hours there thumbing through all the materials and assessing their quality. He could loose himself in the shop and not leave for hours.

He often came across fellow artists, who like him were wandering through the shop, and they would talk at length. The shop assistant would be sent to fetch them coffee from the cafe next door. In the old days they would smoke cigarettes and more besides. Sometimes customers would meander to the back of the shop to find half a dozen bleary eyed artists sitting on stools gesticulating their hands and talking feverishly about art and life.

The shop was run by his friend Jens, the great-great-grandson of the original owner. He had an encyclopedic knowledge of everything in stock. The materials they were made from, where and how they were made, and which artists preferred this or that.

Soon Jens emerged from the store room. 'Hey Peter, what do you need today?' he said.

'I need a large stretched canvas. Two metres wide.'

'You mean a life size canvas, for a figure painting? How exciting. I can prepare one for you in say, two days.'

'No no, I need one right now. I have a vision. I must get it down quickly before it fades. Show me what you have in stock.'

'Yes master, of course, what ever you need.' said Jens.

He took Peter to the store room where he rummaged through prepared canvases that were stacked against the wall. At last he said, 'Ah ha, this is perfect, I will have this one.'

'I'm sorry, you can't take that canvas. It's a special order and it's being collected today.'

Peter glared at Jens, and he understood the urgency.

'But for you master, that customer can wait. What else do you need?'

'Paint, lots of paint.'

He carried the canvas, unwrapped, in both hands with a large bag full of tubes of oil paint back to the studio and struggled up the narrow staircase.

Opening the studio door with his left hand while holding the large canvas in his other he entered and placed the canvas on the easel.

Soon, Elenore arrived and undressed. 'So you are starting the canvas today Peter?' she asked.

'Yes dear, it is time for us to begin in earnest. Please resume the pose.'

Peter had pinned up the various sketches and studies he had made around the room. He picked a soft pencil and looking at Elenore he began to draw her outline on the canvas.

'Oh darling, you look so beautiful today. I'm so looking forward to our big day,' said the painter.

'Our big day? Asked Elenore, 'You mean when the painting is finished?'

Peter didn't seem to hear her but kept mumbling to himself. His face became animated with smiles and frowns. He strained his ear as if he couldn't quite make out what someone was saying, then nodded his head as if he now understood.

All the while Elenore kept her pose. After half an hour Peter said, 'Ten minute rest.'

Peter busied himself mixing paints and choosing brushes. After the break she resumed her pose, and he applied his first strokes of paint to the canvas.

As the afternoon sun began to draw long shadows across the studio and the light slipped away from her body in a sharp dark line. Peter said, 'Enough for today.'

As she was leaving he touched her hand and enveloped her in his arms. 'Darling, you are so wonderful. I can't wait until you return.'

Elenore felt an unease as she walked home. Gregor was waiting for her when she opened the door.

'How did it go today? He asked.

'Peter is progressing fast now. He's started painting the canvas. But now he worries me in a different way. He seems strangely removed. As if he is in another time and place.'

The next morning as Elenore entered the studio, she noticed that the canvas was covered by a sheet.

'You don't want me to see the painting Peter?'

'No my darling, no one can see it until it is finished.'

She resumed her pose and Peter painted.

'Painting is like sculpting in clay,' Peter said, 'You apply a bit here, then there. If you put too much in one place, you take it off and add more where needed. Eventually, the subject emerges. Painting with oil is infinitely malleable, you just keep making changes until you're satisfied.'

'How do you know when you are finished Peter?'

'I never finish a painting. They are simply taken away from me and sold, and I have no further access to them.'

He continued painting, applying layers of light, dark and shadow, filling in the spaces. By the end of the day a definite female form had begun to grow on the canvas.

'Oh darling, I am beginning to see you now, yes you are coming through nicely. You are beautiful my love.'

Elenore had been holding the same pose for two days now and her mind kept drifting off. She had to reminded herself periodically where she was. She heard Peter's voice and presumed he was talking to her. But she looked at him and he seemed distant, as if in another place entirely.

'So you are pleased with progress Peter? She said. But he didn't seem to hear her.

'Peter, is it alright if I leave now? It's getting late?'

'Of course darling, you must do what you need to do.'

She stretched and yawned and got up to put her clothes on. Peter didn't stop painting, and when she walked to the door she said, 'Peter, are you well? Are you alright?'

'Oh yes, I haven't been this happy for so long, it's so wonderful to be with you.'

'Do you want me to come back tomorrow or do you have everything you need now Peter?'

'Humm, what? Oh yes, I have everything I need now. I have no need of anything more.'

'Very well then. Perhaps I will come back in a few days to see how you are progressing. What do you say?'

'Of course darling, of course.'

Elenore walked home unsure if Peter had heard what she had said or not.

'How was the painter today?' asked Gregor.

'I'm worried about him. It's as if he's not there at all.'

'So the painting has stopped?'

'No, on the contrary, he painted furiously all day. He barely took his eyes off the canvas, even when I got up to rest or eat. He didn't seem to notice whether I was there at all. But he kept talking to me. Most of the time I couldn't keep track of what he was saying.'

'Does he want you again tomorrow?'

'No he says he has all he needs now. I said I would go back to check on his progress in a few days.'

'Thank goodness,' said Gregor. I'm glad it's over. I hope the painting turns out to be the masterpiece he wants. How is it looking anyway?'

'I haven't seen it at all. He keeps it covered or turned away from me. He says no one can see it until it's finished.'

'Well he is the painter, and it's his painting,' said Gregor.

7

Peter didn't notice that Elenore had left him. He kept painting, adding a stroke here and another there. He mixed colours on his pallet and applied a few strokes to the face or arm. Now he could see her, yes she was all there. Her smile, so sweet but sad. Her eyes had a different smile than her lips, and he realised, Of course, this was before, yes she was happy then. So changed the lips to match the eyes.

Her breasts were small now, but she was still a young woman, not a mother. Youth is to be enjoyed, and we still have so much time, he thought. He stopped to make him self dinner and ate sitting at his table staring at her, Lana. She was talking to him. It was so nice to hear her voice.

As he finished his meal and washed his plates, he heard her scolding him. She was angry now. He put down the plate and went back to the painting. He changed her eyes, her mouth, the blush on her cheek, the tension in her fingers.

But her anger didn't last, and soon she was happy again. She wanted him, lusted after him. He changed her again. Her mouth drooped down with parted moist lips. Her eyes lost in a fog of desire, passion.

Now they were in a post amorous daze, as if in a cloud. All feeling of self trans-joined in one another. One being, floating in clouds of bliss.

The painter awoke the next morning. He had no recollection of going to bed, only being with his lover entwined in her body. Her fragrant loamy scent enveloped him, his desire stirred again. But where was she? Then he heard her voice and returned to the painting.

'Ah, there you are my love. You are radiant today.'

But then she was angry again and he couldn't bear it, he snapped and shouted at her. Tormented he turned away and she was gone. 'No, no, you cannot leave me can you?'

Her soft voice soon spoke to him again. Relieved, he vowed that they would never be apart again.

Relaxed now, he continued to paint. Life flowed through her and days, months and years of time passed with each stroke of paint he applied. She matured and their lives together grew rich, full of texture and meaning. They understood each other completely and were as one.

Peter savoured his meals, sipped wine in the evening, and talked to Lana into the small hours until his eyes could stay open no more and he slept. The next morning he woke again to find his love still on the canvas and took up his brush and continued to paint.

Lost in time, wrapped in bliss. Peter persisted until with one final stroke, he stopped. He marvelled at the beauty of his painting. The sophistication of his technique. He had captured everything that Lana's life had been, her feelings of joy and loss, meaning and disenchantment. In every line of her beautiful face he could see how the years had left their marks on her. But she had come through all adversity and lived her life to the full. Here she was, perfection, beautiful, vivacious, tender and loving.

Exhausted, his empty wine glass slipped from his hand and still sitting in his chair in front of his finished masterpiece he fell into a deep slumber. Happy that at last he had achieved his goal.

Elenore had told the Museum that she was unwell and could not go to work. Having no idea how many sessions Peter would need her for, she was relieved that after only a few days she could return to her normal schedule. Gregor told her not to worry about the painter, he had a wife who would be looking after him. But as the days went by she never lost the sensation of his eyes burning her skin, his soft hands caressing her, his lips on hers.

Three days went by, and she could wait no more. After work, instead of cycling straight home she peddled over to the studio and walked up the stairs. Ding dong, the doorbell chimed. But there was no answer. She pressed her ear to the door, and she was sure she could hear talking. She rang the bell again but still no answer. She knocked on the door, and again. She listened once more. Could she hear voices, or was it her imagination?

She cycled the rest of the way home her heart pounding again, like the day the painter ignored her and hurt her.

'Gregor, I went to see Peter but he didn't answer the door,' she said.

'He didn't answer the door, or he wasn't there?'

'I think I heard voices, but I'm not sure.'

'Then don't worry Elenore, he's probably with his wife.'

After their evening meal Elenore told Gregor that she was going for a walk. She could not put Peter out of her mind, and she made her way back to the studio. She knocked and rang the bell, but there was still no response. She left confused, not knowing what to do.

She wasn't sure of the address, but when she found the street she remembered and made her way up to Elke's apartment.

She rang the bell but there was no answer there either. As she was leaving a neighbour came out of the apartment next door.

'If you are looking for Elke I am afraid that she is away for a few days,' the woman said.

'Is her husband with her do you know?' asked Elenore.

'I don't think so young lady. I believe that she has gone to Paris on her own.'

Elenore rushed back home.

'Gregor, we must find the painter, I'm so worried about him.'

'I have his phone number. I'll call him,' said Gregor.

He tried the number, but it seemed to be disconnected. Gregor rolled his eyes and said, 'Alright, we'll go to the studio together, but not now, it's too late. We'll go in the morning.'

Elke looked forward to her regular trips to Paris. She had visited several of her favourite dealers and showed them photographs of Peter's completed works from the past year. As always, they agreed to take his work in consignment that they were confident they would sell quickly.

She had telephoned Peter soon after she had arrived and he seemed perfectly fine. He said the model was very professional and that the sessions were going well. She called again the next day, and the day after and he said the same thing. But for the last three days he had not answered the telephone at all, despite her many calls.

She cut short her trip and took an early morning train from Paris to Amsterdam. The train pulled into Amsterdam Central, she made her way outside and found the number 4 tram which stopped very close to Peter's place. Soon Elke was dragging her roller bag up the stairs to the studio.

She was surprised to see a young couple waiting there with worried expressions on their faces.

'Oh, Elke I am so glad you have come. Please excuse us. We were at your soirée last week. Elenore has been modelling for Peter as I am sure you know.'

Elke looked Elenore up and down, 'You are beautiful young lady. At least my husband has taste, um, as do you ...?'

'Oh, I am Gregor, at your service.'

'Have you rung the bell?' Asked Elke?

'Yes, that's why I brought Gregor with me this time. I knocked and rang the bell yesterday and just now but he hasn't come to the door,' said Elenore.

'Allow me,' said Elke, taking out her key and opening the door.

Elke entered the studio and saw Peter slumped in his chair. She rushed to him, but was relieved.

'He's only asleep, the old fool. It seems as if he's been drinking,' she said, looking at the empty wine bottle and fallen glass. 'It's best to just let him sleep, he hasn't touched alcohol in ages.'

The three of them stood in a semicircle around the painter looking down on him. Elenore wanted to take his hand, but she held back sheepishly.

'Was it you that drove him to take up drinking again Elenore?' asked Elke.

'I, I don't know. The last sitting was a few days ago he was working furiously on the painting. He said he didn't need me any more. But he was acting very strangely, talking to himself.'

'Well, lets see how he got on with the painting,' said Elke.

They turned to look at the painting. The morning sun illuminated the studio in a perfect soft light. The large canvas was placed on the easel, and it was covered in paint.

There were dark areas and light areas. The middle section had a large thickness of grey green paint with a multitude of different strokes as if layer upon layer had been added. Perhaps there were many colours, but they had all merged into a soupy melange each one cancelling the other out.

They peered into the mass of paint, trying to discern what was there. They inched closer and closer, tiptoeing, gazing intently at the painting.

'There,' said Elenore, pointing at the canvas, 'Can't you see it? It's a smile, the one he liked the other day. He said that was the look he needed.'

Gregor and Elke peered at the painting.

Gregor said 'Oh yes, you're right, a smile, humm.'

'Ah,' said Elke. 'Yes, I can see it now, a smile.'

****

The Painter

Sean De Siun spent his early years in Australia before moving to London in the early 1970s.

His written works include non fiction redactions, documentaries, screenplays and short stories. He currently lives with his wife in Sydney Australia.

Also by the author and available
from Fileata Fiction

Kings Road
Desire
Caanice and the Book
The Curator
Katie
Chatter

Copy Sales
The Curator is available on **www.amazon.com**
Purchase direct from **www.fileata.co**